THE BOSCH

A NOVELLA

BY

NEAL ASHER

THE BOSCH

Yoon swims towards the lake of the Progenitors. It is forty miles away and, though she vaguely knows the figure, it means little to her. She encompasses the world and it lies within her and, while she looks youthful and fresh, the silver hairs on her head number her years. Conventional time and distance measures of the base-format humans are not useful to her.

In the pellucid waters of the tail lake she ceases swimming, a stream of silver bubbles rising from her lips. She surfaces and strokes leisurely for a shore, stones touch her feet, ribbons of pink and emerald weed brush her legs as she stands and walks up onto a beach of nacre and limestone sand, scattered with the jewelled shells of ammonites and brown carapaces shed by moulting trilobites. She takes a long breath through her nose and on the out-breath ejects the water from her lungs, then looks up at the sky. Evening twilight has rendered it in shades of deep violet and blue, some stars showing between swathes of dark cloud. She can feel something out there that is not immediately visible, but her senses range and connect, and she gazes with her whole self.

An object like a child's spinning top hangs in orbit, scaled with the mica flecks and protruding numerous spines like the sensory tendrils of her trilobites. Around it other objects attach and float as if this thing might be infested with amphipod parasites. She feels an almost nostalgic twist of recognition that links to large portions of her mind that have remained inert for so long, then a partial connection within that raises the spectres of words of definition and communication.

Non-recognition of another object, nearby, or far – she cannot tell – draws her attention. *Stone*. The word rises into her consciousness attaching mental threads to the world around her, then begins to fade for lack of context, thought somewhere inside she knows it is not quite right. With the whole of her perception she sees it flake off part of itself, which drifts across towards the first object, as she sits on the sand, picks up a shell to study its intricacies. Those inert portions of her mind now shift and seek to draw her attention, her connection. Suppressing this seems to take more effort than before, and such is her concentration that too late does she realise she is no longer alone.

The body shell of the first figure flickers with cooling rings she briefly recognises as the aftereffects of concealment. They appear above the short mud and slate cliff at the back of her small beach even as she stands, brushing the sand from her behind. They make noises and she sees in them the shape of her own reflection in still water and of the others of the world, but deep inside knows they are not of the world. One of those portions of her mind springs open like a spring flower, and sounds and shape take on meaning.

'Looks like we got ourselves one,' says a man with skull of polished opal and a face all ridges and whorls, as the other four come up behind him. Three are men with cropped hair rainbow coloured from underlying tattoos. Their shell coverings have a tight almost organic look and black sheen. The woman with them, for Yoon now recognises her as such, is slim elfin and sickly pale, and wears a glassy carapace over some other sand-coloured material. When she grins she reveals the fangs of a snake.

Yoon looks to the lake, uncomfortable with this encounter, ready now to return to the waters and flee old knowledge rising in her mind, but the big man raises an object. Bright flashes scar purple across her vision and punch down into the depths behind her raising explosions of steam. With just a slight whine she knows issue from his covering he jumps down, feet thumping deep into the sand. The woman follows, leaping way over both their heads to land ankle deep in the water, and turns to point another object at Yoon's face. Threat is evident, but any kind of response is not. She just stares at them.

'Nothing to say?' asks the man.

Word meanings flicker in her skull. She continues studying them, identifying objects and actions in a growing lexicon: *armour, laser carbine, snake gun, servo assist,* while the three in black she identifies as *Batian mercenaries.* But these float in a gulf of incomprehension. She makes a noise – a rusty croaking from vocal cords so long unused – and words of response dart like fishes from her grasp.

He reaches out fast and grabs her forearm, fingers closing with bruising force. Dropping his carbine to hang from its strap he pulls a manacle attached by a chain to his belt and closes it about her wrist.

3

'Sure you can handle her, Ibruk?' says one of the Batians, which seems a source of amusement to the others.

The man, Ibruk, glances at the Batian and shows what seems to be overdramatic annoyance, then tugs on the chain. She follows him across the strand. Danger is here and she becomes aware she must act. She stoops, comes up with a handful of sand and throws it in his face. As he flinches back she reaches down with her free hand and crushes the manacled one, bone and gristle crunching, pain intense. Slipping the manacle free she leaps for the water, but the pale glass-armoured woman hits her mid-flight and they fall to the shallows. Yoon claws at her opponent, toxin-laced nails sliding off glass. With a hiss the albino's jaws open too wide and she bites. Yoon recognises the poison flooding in even as the paralysis spreads and unconsciousness ensues.

Sunlight beams in through the cave mouth. Rage rises up inside Yoon around blank spots in her mind, like burns too painful to touch. But she knows she has been violently assaulted. Wounds penetrate through her wrists and ankles, broken bones grate against each other sending sick waves of pain through her, skin and muscle are torn and bruised and her poisoned claws have been ripped out. Aware that the assault extended beyond these injuries, she lies in filth with blood leaking from her vagina. A ball of pain sits between her legs, while four compartments of her womb have closed about distinct seed so violently expended.

Yoon sits up, slowly stands, and makes her way out into the sunlight. She gazes longingly at the waters beyond the strand. But she cannot return, not now, the anger and the insult require response, and to respond, she must return to all of herself. Urgency is also a factor, because the perpetrators were not of the world and so might depart it. She dips her head and closes her eyes, internal vision upon her simplified mind that even now is becoming more complex because some of those inert portions strain for activation. Reaching into herself she also reaches out, to the world and its storage. Fragments of mentality open and connect. Memory rises:

Yoon opens her eyes, aching all over, teeth broken in her mouth. She recognises the cave by the fossil clams in the roof and the yellow and green calcite streaking the walls. It is not far from where they captured her. Further pain makes itself known and she looks aside at her manacled wrist. They have pulled her claws and ensured the manacles cannot come free by dint of spikes driven through them and her wrists. They have chained her spread eagled – all manacles similarly fixed and their chains leading to pegs hammered into the floor.

'And it's just this?' says one of the Batians. 'A punishment?'

'Does it bother you?' asks the snake woman.

'Just seems a lot of effort, but you pay so you say.'

Yoon clamps down on that. She is not ready to encompass the rest because in her simplified state it might break her. Instead she circumvents recent memory and slides into what went before. The century of just living in the world, without complex thought, rolls away and all her previous life begins to fall into place. She drops to her knees, weakened by blood loss certainly, but mostly by a history her mind cannot contain and does not contain, for it is etched into her world. Millennia of memory open to her. Time passes, but now she can measure it. Within this she finds the correct responses, the old responses, and the necessities.

Yoon stands and with her whole self she gazes at the sky. The first object she earlier saw from this beach resolves as a space station five miles across that has sat there for longer than living memory – for most living memory. The amphipods are the ships of the traders, travellers and seekers of novelty, docked around this structure, or in the process of arriving or leaving, here to bring the beads and toys they hope to exchange for the biologicals her people make, only to learn that hard currency or transfers to the her world bank will do. This is all as usual but, as she noted in her more simplified state, something else has come.

Yes, it looks to be made of stone but is almost certainly some other material. The mega-ship is a frozen thick-armed orrery, or perhaps gimbals for there are no representations of worlds or moons in it. It is opaque to her as so many things are not, and a curiosity. Those aboard looking down on her home will see the Mandelbrot patterns of lakes across its surface, each swirl of them like, as someone once said, a string of anal beads coiled on itself. The object she saw flake away was a shuttle heading to the station, but it is no longer there and she traces it down to the surface – to the human city and its space port. Perhaps, despite being docked to the station all the while, this arrival has something to do with the attack upon her? She flinches away from that as suppressed memory threatens to rise. No matter. Her law is what it is and she will act as she acts.

Aware now of the extent of herself, and the facilities of the body she wears, she powers up the organic circuitry in her skull and reaches out to the space station and works around the connections to an AI long turned to dust to find the warden. He is a descendent of the family that has ruled there for millennia – the dregs of a human polity that either no longer exists, or has moved on somewhere else. Though his cerebral additions are mechanistic, contact establishes quickly. He recognises her at once even though his grandfather was the last she spoke to there.

'It is you,' he says. 'Rumours were that you died long ago.'

'I am alive,' she says. 'What ships have departed the surface in the last ten hours?'

'None, goddess,' he replies. Even through his primitive cerebral implants she feels his desperation to speak further – to expand the contact – and his frustration with the long-established protocols that do not permit this.

'Allow none to depart until I give permission – there has been an incident,' she tells him.

'This is . . . unexpected. The rules are understood. What sort of incident?'

'I have been assaulted and the culprits must make restitution.'

'Assaulted! You!' His shock breaks the contact for a moment, but then he comes back with, 'If you could give me detail on the assailants. . .'

'That will not be necessary. Now tell me about the new vessel?' she enquires.

'A new Krodor ambassador has arrived and, like so many, of course seeks audience.'

'On what matters?' As she asks this she acknowledges a connection, for the man Ibruk is a krodorman.

'He did not feel inclined to tell me.'

'He will have to wait.'

'Many have been waiting for a very long time,' he observes.

'And they will have longer to wait yet,' she replies, the hint of reprimand in her tone.

'Your will,' the Warden agrees quickly. 'Can I assist you in other matters?'

She decides to throw him a bone. 'When I have dealt with this particular matter I will contact you again.' Then she breaks the link.

Yoon walks across the sand to the water, and wades in. Human time and distance are a factor here so she will not swim all the way to the Progenitors. Her rapists will be in the city and unable to leave now she has given her orders. The Warden will inform all those below and, if that is not enough, use station weapons against any who try to depart. However, the rape was so calculated; the knowledge of the response so widely understood. There must be machinations behind it, escape routes and contingency plans and human politics she cannot yet parse. She pauses, remembering the response of this Ibruk to one of the Batians, and surmises that either he did not want his name spoken, or he wanted her to know that he did not want it spoken. There is some subterfuge here she cannot yet see. Yoon grimaces. No matter. The Progenitor must come first and events will proceed from there. Placing her hand the water, she swirls it, blood dissolving and spreading a message already written.

Next diving in, she swims out and tends to other needs. Internal vision gives the extent of the wounds and accelerated response raises her body temperature until hot swirls of water depart her skin. Her finger ends close and generate new nails, peaking through with curved points, muscle reforming until she can extend them a half inch from her fingertips. Inside her vagina, tears heal and knit. Bruises darken and shrink leaving yellow in their wake, and that fades. Abrasions shudder, shedding slivers of dead skin.

She focuses on her belly, seeing carvings there in some opaque script. A scrap of memory surfaces and integrates before she can stop it:

  . . . *the pale woman is the worst, carving patterns on her belly with a glass knife and playing with herself the while. . . Finally it is over. The woman looks up to Ibruk, who stands expressionless. She nods to herself then bites, and Yoon's world goes away. . .*

Yoon shudders back into the present and the practicalities of her aims. No seed from the woman – no source of a Bosch – but Yoon will find her. She closes the cuts on her belly and erases what the *albino ophidapt* woman wrote. In her womb Yoon holds miserly onto the precious cargos, separate and living. Breathing water she hangs in clear depths, dives to bivalves, sheep-huddled on the bottom, waves a hand over them and they open. She pulls out their offering of flesh leaving the living and soon-to-regenerate animal behind, feasts under water and steadily renews her resources. Finally she surfaces and sees the great fin approaching. A Progenitor has come, sensitive to her blood, great mouth agape and full of triangular teeth, the great white shark of its ancestry writ large: one of the engines of the biology of her world.

Kicking water she waits until it passes close, one of the human arms growing from behind its lower jaw reaching out and brushing her with shark skin fingers. Turning, she swims with it for a while then reaches out and clasps the big hand, towed along by the shark. Gently, rhythmically in the language of touch and timing, she strokes its side in four distinct areas. The shark shudders with pleasure – the message reaching down through its nervous system and eliciting the expected response. Its tail stops flicking and it shudders again. The egg package – a worm with four clear spheres inside – oozes out of its back end and twitches in the current of the next flick of its tail. She releases her hold as the shark turns. Sculling back to the package she cups it in her palm. It is smaller than her little finger. Bringing it down between her legs she pushes it into the mouth of her vagina and feels it eagerly squirm inside. She tracks its progress to her compartmentalised womb where it implants each egg, its body deflating to a wisp that will fall out of her later. Fertilization is marked by four small shocks transmitted through her autonomics, and ensuing growth is fast and hot. She doesn't know what Bosches this will produce, though she can guess and knows they will be appropriate, and swims down to the clams again to feed the process.

She eats and burns, heating the water around her again as she did during healing. Her stomach bubbles with strong acid quickly digesting the clam protein, fats and minerals. Blood runs thick to her endometrium as eggs grow fast into masses of cells and then zygotes enwrapped in fleshy cauls. Her torso expands as she swims to the surface to breathe oxygen and recharge her cells, for that in the water is not enough. Swimming down again she clutches clamshell and squats. Her underwater moans send away a shoal of ammonites in inkjet panic. Trilobites that had been attracted by the debris from her feeding scuttle away too. She dilates, moaning still, and the first zygote sac slides out, trailing cord, then the next and the next, sticking themselves to the bottom. She rests for a while before dispelling the fleshy placenta. They will feed on that after they have eaten their cauls. A wave of her hand and its output of pheromones open clams on the bottom all across the lake. The same pheromone brings the crustaceans and molluscs back, and then catfish, black tuna and shoals of other fishes. None of these feed though there is food aplenty. They are bent to her will and waiting – food themselves. She swims for the shore.

Yoon pulls herself from the water, sniffs the air to detect the drift of cooking smoke. She must prepare now to venture into civilization and, for that, she must first go to her own people. They have not seen her up close for some decades, and even back then just a simplified creature swimming the tail lakes, but they always remember because she is written into their code.

Petod and Imhran threat display, their ink flushing blooms of red against the intricate blue, and sometimes orange fire in the charcoal skeletons of buildings. They circle closer and closer to violence, muscles taut and oiled and sweating the hormones of sex. They have drunk the Progenitor milk as is custom, but their genetics are not customary. Lactose intolerance takes its toll as they stamp and gesticulate. Imhran farts like a fog horn and Petod replies with the drawn-out quack of a duck dobblering past. Their tense expressions twist as they segue into the ridiculous, fall together in giggles and guffaws and collapse to the dust.

The tribe is disappointed by the lack of injury and subsequent demonstrations of self-healing. Females shrug amusement at yet another mating fight without conclusion. All move away – some to their cyst houses, others out into the Fen and still others taking the road to the city, loaded down with packs of biologicals for the off-worlders. Petod smiles to himself.

'They'll want us to fight again,' Imhran observes.

Petod collects his folded clothing from a rock. He pulls on underwear, heat-weave combats and heavy boots, an ever-white shirt and a chromic jacket with many pockets – its colour set to match the beige and green camouflage of the combats. Imhran dresses too, but in a simple toga and sandals.

'We defy convention by our actions but first with our biology,' says Petod. He then tilts a head to the wild-side border of the village. 'What's this?'

'Primitive,' says Imhran, but there is doubt in his voice.

The woman is completely naked, very attractive and silver haired. Something nags at Petod and a surge of feeling like nostalgia runs through his body. A smell, at once familiar and alien reaches his nostrils. Peripherally he sees villagers turning, dropping packages or ceasing their tasks and beginning to walk towards the woman. She continues in as the first of them reaches her, goes down on his knees and touches her arm as she passes. Others do the same, but all stand afterwards and follow her in. He can see expressions of joy, fear and awe, while tears run from many eyes. Intellectually he sees only the woman, but the half of his bastard biology that is this world recognises her first, his intellect slowly catching up.

'It is Yoon,' says Imhran, voicing what Petod accepts only a moment later.

Her gaze swings towards them and she walks over. She looks them up and down. Imhran she both dismisses and accepts with a touch that leaves him shaking with his head bowed. She turns to Petod.

'You live in the city,' she says.

He nods mutely.

She does not raise her voice but it carries now. 'I have been assaulted by off-worlders. I am raising Bosch and must go to the city.'

A muttering angry rumble passes through the crowd which, Petod sees, is now the whole of the village. Bosch? Legendary monsters? Assaulted? She turns back to him.

'I will need clothing, weapons and whatever other accoutrements of their civilization are required to pass amongst them unnoticed.'

13

'You have no power over me,' Petod manages, rebellion rising from the genome of his off-world mother, and he sees hostile gazes turn towards him. 'I don't believe the legends.'

'But. . .' she says, and that is all.

She smiles and holds out a hand. A woman has brought her a skin-tight heat-weave bodysuit, which she takes and hangs over her shoulder. A man brings a case of weapons. Other items appear around her, laid at her feet like offerings. She makes her selections, exchanges badinage as if she is a villager herself. Thanks them and dispatches them away from her with a touch. She pulls on the suit, straps a Cougar on her hip, and drops spare clips for the gun and gifts of food into a pack.

'The Bosch will be rising soon,' she says, as villagers drift away. 'I must see them and accept them, then I go into the city to hunt down my attackers. I understand their world, but a guide and a companion may bring me focus.'

She gazes at Petod expectantly, but he does nothing. She nods and, turning, heads out of the village. *There,* thinks Petod. *You have no power over me.* He returns to the cyst house he has shared with Imhran during this visit home. Imhran is peeling blue potatoes and staring out the window.

'Well that was interesting,' says Petod.

Imhran turns to him, his smile beatific. Petod recognises a sense of something. He feels he is facing one of the villagers rather than his brother. The cyst house seems suddenly claustrophobic and he can feel some truth, sliding out of his compass. He turns and heads to his room, gathers his things and puts them in his backpack – swiftly done because he is always ready to leave on short notice when those he grew up with come, as they always do, to baffle him.

'You are going back to the city?' Imhran asks.

'I am. She can find someone else.'

'Who can find someone else?' Frown lines appear. Perhaps he thinks he has forgotten some anecdote Petod related about the city. This is common because Imhran shows only polite interest.

Petod waves vaguely. 'It's not important.'

The frown lines disappear. 'Stay safe.'

'Yes, that's always best.' Petod steps to the door knowing the sarcasm is lost on his brother.

Outside, Petod huffs cool air, then brushes one arm to bring up a screen in the tattoos there, briefly scans messages then checks the time. Two hours to sundown, so he can reach Trelland Station well before and be in his favourite bar before darkness. Legends of monsters intimate that bright light and company might be a good choice. He begins walking, that image in his mind to cheer him, then slowly fading as reality impinges. He's following her, of course.

Yoon sits on the beach where the mercenaries first found her and watches the lake. Its surface is boiling with activity. A giant salmon leaps only for a long double-jointed arm to spear up and snatch it in a clawed hand. It disappears out of sight when she feels him come to the low cliff at the back of the beach, and the sensation is too familiar. A flash of emotion, parts anger, fear and humiliation raises hot sweat on her skin. She reaches down and touches the Cougar at her hip, gains some control but does not withdraw her hand. The weapon is a vicious thing with a clip of one thousand metallic hydrogen micro-beads with cores of diamond-pressed super-oxide. Each bead has devastating penetrating power and is explosive. She knows the weapon as intimately as much Old Polity technology, having been long acquainted with it. Had she such a gun to hand things would have gone very differently with the mercenaries. Had she the awareness then that she has now, the weapon would not have been necessary at all. He jumps down, landing clumsily and walks out to stand next to her.

'I am a bastard by-blow of base-format and your people,' he says. 'My mother was a xenobiologist and my father a man who denied the tenets. I am an abomination.'

She gazes at him, taking in his youth and naivety, the biology at war within him, and at last, mentally separating him from her attacker, withdraws her hand from the gun and pats the sand at her side. 'Sit down.'

She senses rebellion rise inside him, precisely countered by his tie to her world. Neither wins the battle and, as expected, it is curiosity that brings him down by her side.

'We originals came here to make our biotech paradise,' she says, 'and incorporated our rules and our ways into our biology. Natural law. By and by my fellows died through mischance and boredom, while their children, and mine, grew and flourished. Some live for centuries, some do not, all are in tune with the world so see no problem in returning to it. I returned once but need recalled me when the Polity came. I perforce had to make rules of engagement with the outsiders. While reacting to them, my people made their own rules and mores.'

'I don't understand.' He gazes at her, frown lines deep.

'The mores of the society that raised you are their own, not mine. They may call you bastard, by-blow or abomination, but I do not. And even now the people question those mores in the face of change.'

He grimaces, then points out to the lake. 'What's there?'

'Bosch,' she replies.

Something is now swimming towards the shore and she can see his fear. He may well have inserted himself into the society of the city, but his genetic memory remains uncorrupted by additional biology.

'When the Polity went away others, of a rougher kind from other places, came here and still come. I had to meet their violence with my own and gave them a lesson in fear. From time to time the lesson must be reinforced.'

A walnut brown head breaches the surface followed by wide muscular shoulders. In the shallows the swimmer heaves itself up and stands. Bird eyes blink in the bird skull, long ibis beak protruding. Of course it must be the Plague Doctor first, it always is. This is a form she favours though it doesn't strictly arise from the art of an ancient painter. It walks up the beach on bird feet to stand before her. She touches its small mind briefly and it moves off to one side to crouch in the sand where it picks up ammonite shells in clawed fingers and then breaks them.

'I never believed, not really,' says Petod. His arms are wrapped around his knees and he is shivering, though the evening is not cold.

The Cowfish leaves the lake, white as ivory, hooves thumping, two stunted bat wings flapping behind an armless torso, tongue the tentacle of an octopus writhing in a carp's gape around which barbles dangle. It hisses, folds its wings and goes to its fellow, there to sketch strange shapes in the sand with its tongue. Catape then comes – a thin humanoid with fingers like spider legs, clad in beige fur, fanged ape mouth and cat's eyes in an earless head. The Bird comes last, a striding shoebill with a mouth so much wider and lined with blunt teeth, feathers ragged and oily. Yoon assesses them all as they squat on the sand. Even though the memories of the act remain blocked, she knows their respective sources. The last three are the offspring of the Batian mercenaries while, of course, the Plague Doctor she has engendered from the seed of the mercenary Ibruk. She has nothing for the albino woman, and everything. These creatures are hers to command and will kill who she chooses, in whatever manner she chooses. They will just not reach *completion* in the act if the victim is not their father.

'The Bosch,' she says.

'You're going to walk into the city with those?' Petod asks shakily.

She waves a hand and, responding to the pheromone instruction, the Bosch draw the night in around them. She can see them, as if through a lens darkly, but knows that to Petod they have faded into shadow.

18

'Now we will go to the city,' she says. 'And you will show me where to search.'

Petod walks at her side shooting occasional glances at her. So utterly normal to him – in a glance just a human woman of ancient Asiatic descent with long silver hair – but viscerally her mere presence nags at him. He feels he must be aware of her needs and ready to respond, or at least, acknowledge them, and it all seems like a demand for obeisance. Yet, when he manages to step back from the feelings they seem like love, and he hates that. He knows what drives this: she is the expression of the world of which he is part. She calls to his very biology, to elicit deep responses: arousal engendered from the perfect mate, the hunger of a starving man, but also the prey's fear of a predator and its feeling of inevitability once captured. He turns away, confused and groping for rationality.

Away from the village and the lakes they now walk the gloom of deep Fen. The sun sets in amber fire and the stars blink crystal spider eyes. Stands of rat-tails and tree fern loom over them while ball moss and grass soften the edges of the flaked stone path. Here and there grow fungi – their bright colours muted by the twilight. He sees bald rabbits scuttling away, eyes wide with panic, because of the things that walk off the path. He cannot see the Bosch clearly for they shift shadow, and is glad not to. Just the hiss of skin or fur against plants and the squelch of damp moss, elicits a primal fear arising from his genetics, and from legend. The Bosch are punishers of aberrant children, monsters lurking in the night, soul suckers and diners on human flesh. In the villages they truly believe in them, but also in the justice of them so, oddly, fear is diminished there. In the city where tough urbanites dismiss fable, many wear ward charms and check the shadows in the night. Real fear lives in the alleys and tenements because those same urbanites feel maybe they are unjust, and deserving of the punishment of the Bosch.

'They won't harm you,' says Yoon, 'unless you stand in the way of their purpose.'

'If you say so.' He tries to be sarcastic but finds, in his heart, he means it.

The path winds on through the Fen as night falls. The Green Moon rises, lighting their way with reflection from the labyrinthine ruins that wrap it. Talk of reoccupying the place has led nowhere, for its haunted reputation makes people reluctant to sign up for the chore. Yoon and Petod climb a low hill in the Spineland between curved lines of lakes and gaze down from a flat stone slab,

'Trelland Station,' he says, almost proudly.

She turns and smiles. 'I know – I did give my permission for this.'

He nods, remembering school time histories of when the Polity came. Establishing their space station they began their explorations and interventions on the surface, but Yoon ejected them and it seemed used the Bosch then. By and by she allowed an embassy on the surface. Trade, useful to her people, ensued, and the embassy acquired a space port, then further land for expansion, which in time resulted in the walled city. She next, this being five hundred years ago, allowed the railway, running through the Spinelands and webbing around the city for a thousand miles. He supposed she felt it a small intrusion on an entire world. The city, named Foothold, is only called The City by its dwellers. It unlikely they will see another one in their lifetimes they feel no need to give it distinction.

They take the winding path down towards the terminal building – two long low structures like a barrel split lengthwise and folded down on the ground. Lights shine out of the open ends to reveal the line itself, or rather two lines – like pipes split lengthwise and cupping upwards. To prevent growth or wildlife encroaching and being damaged, and not to prevent problems for the trains, she specified this style of maglev all those centuries ago.

Soon the path widens, pin-lights on slim poles marking its way through a stand of pineapple cycads. Flaked stone gives way to plasticrete as they approach the arched doors to the first building. Petod can hear the hum of the lev and knows, as per the schedule, that a train is inside. Through the archway now he can see it – a long slim vehicle with its ramp doors closed up – departure not imminent. He pauses at one of the ticket posts then looks round at her.

'We must buy tickets.' He peers back at vaguely seen shapes in the gloom. He throws his hands up, not sure what she will do now, then waves a tattoo over the reader. 'The City,' he says.

'Number of passengers?' the post enquires. He turns to her again.

'Don't concern yourself. I will buy my own,' she tells him.

'One ticket,' he tells the post, and it extrudes a small slip of paper etched with circuitry like the runes of a mathematical deity. He walks through, up to the base of the steps leading to the platform, and turns to watch.

Yoon gazes at the post for a moment whereupon it issues five tickets. Organic circuitry, he realizes, and falls into speculation on that. In so many ways she is this world and exerts control all around her of its biology, but also of the degrading technology of the city and the space station. She walks through to join him and shadows slide in from the Fen. The Bosch lose part of their disguise, perhaps because it cannot confuse the strong lights here. All speculations flee his mind as the Plague Doctor steps out of the night. It now wears clothing of a sort: a long cape from neck to foot. The others come similarly attired and somehow, because of this and because of the remaining shadow that clings around them, binding them together as one, they seem all the more monstrous.

'Where did they get those?' he asks.

'I cast ahead to maker fungi,' she replies. 'They dug up their garments while we travelled.'

'Oh, right.'

Her connection with the world. Cloth, made from the tough mycelia of certain fungi, is an item of trade, but the villagers nurture the fungi, program them with pheromones and run the mycelia through growing-looms. Here she has made something with a thought, through the organic circuitry of her body.

Stooped down and trailing shadow the Bosch follow as she and he mount the steps. Petod moves quickly ahead, looking each way along the platform.

Villagers here carry packs or stand by wheeled carts, waiting until cleaning robots have made their sweeps of each carriage. Also here are some from the city – easily identifiable by their clothing. On the opposite platform the same mix of people is making its way towards the middle exit from the two buildings.

'This is going to be interesting,' he opines, spine crawling with the Bosch at his back.

He heads towards the train, halting behind the line that marks where the ramp doors come down. People turn towards them and he hears exclamations of surprise and fear. Some villagers begin to approach, drawn as they were back in his home village, but their pace loses impetus, and they halt with hands raise to mouths or clutching amulets. They begin to fade back. In a group of four city dwellers, one in body armour swears at a fellow and pushes him away, then turns and resolutely begins striding down the platform. But his belligerent pace loses impetus too as what he dismissed as foolish fable gradually reveals its truth. He becomes hesitant, but pushes himself on. The Plague Doctor rears up with claws protruding from its fungus robes. The man's mouth gapes and he pales as he halts. After a moment, he waves a dismissive arm and heads back to his fellows.

'Best we get on.' Petod steps to a lowering ramp now the cleaning robots stow themselves under the train seats. Others here move as far away from this carriage as they can. He climbs the ramp and looks back, in time to see Yoon handing out tickets to each of the Bosch. Two of them do not have hands, but clamp them in, respectively, a mouth and a beak. She follows him in and the creatures flow up behind her. He sits and she sits next to him while the Bosch move to occupy the carriage area designated for trade goods and other luggage. With the rattle of aged hydraulics the ramp doors close. A low hum crescendos and the train pulls out into the dark, lights spearing ahead to scare away anything on the maglev. He waits, watching the green glint of the lakes in the moonlight, and notes hints of blood as Red Moon begins its rise. Fen speeds by for some while, during which Petod again questions his choices and motivations.

'She is taking her time,' he eventually says.

'Who?' Yoon asks.

'The ticket collector.'

'Ah.'

Tickets are not needed, nor ticket collectors or any human staff. This peccadillo of some city official centuries ago gave employment and, to a certain extent, oversight of machines that sometimes do not run so well. Eventually the back door of the carriage opens. A woman in a green uniform, with the cap pulled tight over blond hair, makes a determined approach.

She draws opposite Yoon and Petod. 'Tickets please.'

They oblige and she runs them over her reader, her gaze firmly on the tickets and nothing else. Her hands shake as she passes them back, swallows noisily and moves on. At the Bosch she repeats her mantra, and the Plague Doctor holds out its ticket first. Now as white as salt she can hardly control the palsy of her hands. Ticket scanned, she returns it, then reaches out to take the ticket from the Bird's toothed beak. She takes and reads the next two, then muttering to herself turns back along the aisle. She halts by Yoon and Petod again.

'They were tickets for people. Livestock is much cheaper,' she advises, then moves on down the carriage. Petod admires her resolve not to break into a run to get away.

'Now,' says Yoon. 'Your thoughts on how we must proceed in the city?'

It seems too prosaic to discuss, but he makes an effort.

'First I need to know who you are hunting,' he says.

'Three Batian mercenaries, an albino ophidapt woman and a big Krodorman with a stone skull. They will, I am sure, be in hiding.'

He remembers she had been assaulted – it had passed out of his mind during recent events. He studies her, thinking she does not look like a victim.

'Very well,' he begins. 'First you must acquire hard currency. They will be hiding in the areas of the city where the surveillance system is down, and that usually means where people do not like to be watched and want to keep their transactions secret.'

'The less salubrious quarters?'

'Exactly. You need money for bribes . . . How long do you think this will take?'

'Some days, I imagine – maybe longer.'

'Then you will need to pay for accommodation in such a place too.'

'You do not have any?'

'I rent a room whenever I am in the city, but let it go when I leave.'

'You will join me, then.'

He finds this disconcerting – the idea of living in close proximity with both her and the Bosch. He glances at them again. The Plague Doctor squats by one wall holding a flat slab of rock it scribes with one claw with a sinister clicking and screeing. Cowfish and Bird stand face to face, heads pressing together as if communing, while Catape grooms itself, licking its fur and making a sawing sound like a purr, but like one from the darkness where a big cat is watching.

'A landlord might be a bit reluctant to take you in,' Petod observes.

'The Bosch will not be with us – they will be hunting.'

He nods, seeing just how that will play out in the city. The passengers here will spread the news, if the ticket collector has not already called ahead. People will be understandably fearful.

The train follows the curve of the Spineland giving Yoon a good view of the City through the side window. It rises up out of the landscape, in appearance like a fortified town from unimaginably ancient times. Its population has grown and, because of limits she placed on the city's extent, buildings are packed tightly inside its walls, the streets narrow between and on many levels. She notes that the station now lies outside the walls and other buildings have spilled out around it. She frowns, realizing she has not been paying much attention here over the last century or so. Perhaps she now needs to. She will see.

Briefly now she turns her attention inward, wincing with the effort. Her physical wounds have all but healed but they psychic wounds are still raw and open: five acts, five holes in her mind, four of them extending to the Bosch their closure dependent on the fulfilment of her creatures. The fifth – that of the snake woman – connects them and she senses some truth in that. It will be revealed by and by. She turns her attention outward again.

Beyond the city, half concealed by it, sits the platform of the space port. Numerous gantries and warehouses are scattered there between many ships of various design. Some stand like rockets of old, others are whales beached down on their bellies while the shapes of others defy comparison. She recognizes one grey object, smaller than the rest, as the shuttle of the Krodor ambassador. That presence seems to affirm her need for more involvement here, much as she resents the idea.

The train sweeps round and down its lev line converging with many others entering the station. Another train pulls out of the arch of one half-barrel building and heads away. Numerous platforms lie bright inside where the Bosch will not achieve complete concealment. Almost certainly city officialdom will react, so she must dispatch the Bosch on their way as soon as possible. As the train pulls in towards its own platform, confirmation is the presence of a large crowd, while other platforms stand empty. The train slows and she eyes these people – city dwellers mostly but also many of her own. A man hung in expensive robes and platinum chain must be Mayor Gralson, who has been in office for two decades. She only knows him through her updates from the world. Around him cluster officials in baroque businesswear, but also police in tight grey uniforms, bearing hammer guns and screamer batons.

'This is inconvenient,' she says to Petod.

'The ticket collector must have told them,' he replies. 'They'll want to assist you, while taking the opportunity to use you as an excuse for urban redesign and renewal, which usually means going heavy-handed into those less salubrious areas.'

'I understand.' She reaches out to the Bosch, who immediately put away concerns that are strange artefacts of their tightly-woven mental structures and, as one, turn to face her when she stands.

The train jerks to a halt and ramp doors clatter and wheeze their way to the platform. She considers the utility of these officials and their policemen. Their interference will likely drive her prey deep underground, and confuse an issue that until now had been so clear to her. It has been so long time since she visited here that most of the population, though perhaps born and raised here, are not part of her biology. They may have forgotten, and will resent and possibly rebel against her will. Time to remind them. She instructs the Bosch and they loosen and part internal structures while emitting pheromones. These will at least key into her people and, she realizes when glancing at Petod, those who are partially hers.

'Oh no.' He shrinks down in his seat, his gaze fixed on the Bosch as they expand, bone sliding and cracking against bone, muscles stretching and inflating as their meta-materials reconfigure and mesh. Already the Plague Doctor is stooped over to accommodate his increased height in the carriage. She reaches over and presses a hand against Petod's face, emitting a counteragent to the chemical terror. He slumps, bewildered.

'Go and show them,' she instructs the Bosch.

The Plague doctor heaves itself towards the ramp emitting a shriek across the sound spectrum from ultrasound to infrasound, tuned to clench a fist around fight or flight, driving a surge of adrenaline that tips towards terror. Seeming to slide rather than walk it flows down onto the platform, and out. Already her people are screaming in response and push away in the crowd. The mayor staggers back and goes down on his backside. Hammer guns thump, their shots passing through the Doctor and starring the glass down the side of the carriage, but not penetrating. The Bird reaches the head of the ramp next, wings spread to the full width of the exit, eyes burning as it too shrieks. The Doctor is now amidst the retreating crowd. It picks up one of the shooters and tosses him twenty feet to hit a station pillar and slide down. Guns hammer fire again and again, but the police now guard the retreat of officials. Two policemen haul up the mayor by his armpits and drag him away as the Cowfish slides down, mouth agape. It shoots towards one cop guarding the retreat as he fires into it to no effect. It comes down on him with that mouth and rears up, his legs kicking as it swallows him.

'They are killing,' Petod manages.

She turns to him. 'I am reminding them of the rules. Attack a Bosch and you pay the penalty. Show violence towards me and you pay it too.' She gestures towards the crazed windows even as one of them collapses into pieces. He looks sickened and she cannot understand why this bothers her so.

The Catape is out last, bringing down a straggler and clawing him, shredding his uniform. She links again and delivers instructions. The Catape pulls back and the policeman escapes, bloody but alive. The Plague Doctor releases the two it is holding by their throats up off the ground and they collapse to the platform. After a moment the least injured helps the other away. To one side the Cowfish heaves and regurgitates. The one it swallowed crawls away covered in white slime to where a woman of Yoon's own people helps him up and they too retreat. She eyes the woman, surprised at this control of terror. Something else she must investigate, like much here.

By the time Yoon walks down the ramp all have fled the station, but for one prone figure. Petod follows her, scanning the empty platform – the abandoned belongings and weapons.

'Thank you,' he says.

She shrugs and gestures to the Bosch. 'They will behave similarly with any who turn against them, perhaps this will prevent further injury or death.' But even as she speaks she feels uncomfortable under his gaze. She waves a hand, pheromone instruction already keyed. The Bosch, returned somewhat to their previous scale, pull together mated in shadow. Rather than head for the platform exit they slide across it towards the front of the train, over the edge and along the cupped track towards the end. From there they can gain access to tunnels leading into the city – towards their prey.

Yoon watches them go then walks over to the fallen policeman and stoops down next to him. He is still alive but she can sense him dying. His ribs are crushed and a lung collapsed. She drives a claw into his side, hearing the sharp intake of breath from Petod. With a hiss the man's lung re-inflates. She drives in other claws, injecting her biologicals, killing his pain, spreading repair mechanisms packed into bacteria, tailored viruses and healing chyme. With a heave she shifts him so his back is up against the pillar. He coughs some blood, opens his eyes.

'You are real,' he manages.

'You will live,' she says, and stands. To Petod she says, 'We must go.'

The bank room was without people, the central pillar responding to her touch. She wears her hair tucked up inside a wide-brimmed hat he snatched from the platform but, even so, he can see her hair changing colour – black streaks appearing in the silver he can see. He had suggested concealment with hair dye and new clothing. She told him the dye was unnecessary but the clothing a good idea, but first they needed untraceable currency. His feelings about her are still mixed. At the station she displayed a frightening callousness in someone so powerful, but then, he felt sure in response to his reactions, compassion of a kind.

'I must pay you,' she says.

'Yes,' he agrees. 'You must.'

The touch screen is organic, rippling to her fingers. Organic circuitry runs around the walls like lichen, connecting to nodes of city tech – the whole system integrated. All use her bank because her currency does not fluctuate while the bank's resources are ever growing. Not only does she have godlike powers over the biology of her world, but the power of wealth.

'I have placed a million Clare in your account, but now, as you say, we need hard currency. What is preferred now in those less salubrious areas?'

A million!

He swallows dryly and initiates a connection in the tattoos on his arm, gapes at the truth of his sudden fortune.

'Clare is good,' he manages, 'but also the ReCarth Shilling if you need to pay off-worlders for anything.'

She caresses the screen and a turn box opens in the pillar. This reveals ten one hundred shilling tubes and five one thousand Clare pouches.

'This will be enough?'

'Yes. More than.'

He leads her from the lamp-lit streets of the trade and banking quarter – its bright buildings with their red, green and yellow lights looming above – to a stair winding down into the alleys of the Basement. In a mall lit by fluorescent vines he finds a clothing shop he knows. Eighty Clare buys city wear hooded cloaks with shimmer masks and other garments besides. Suitably concealed they head through the Basement to the stair up into Shadsville. More money spent in a small supermarket on food, drink and other necessities and, loaded down with bags, they move on. He had thought to take her to his home territory but perhaps he was recognized at the station, and perhaps some will be looking, if they dare.

Shadsville lies two levels up from the Basement, but still doesn't open to the sky. The foundations of buildings above are the angled scaffolds of a roof where night birds and gargoyle bats roost – their droppings an ever present annoyance in the streets below. It is a place of tenements, bars, gaming rooms, curiosity shops and those for illegal biologicals. The tenement he chooses leans out at an angle into the street – six floors of dusty oval windows and doors behind a complex matrix of platforms and stairs all tangled in blue ivy and sweet peas from numerous pots and troughs. They enter a foyer and approach a service window. A morose fat man stands up from an array of circular soft screens and comes to the window.

'Your best apartment – two beds please,' says Petod.

'Pay up front,' says the man. 'Cash only – fifty Clare a night.'

'Three nights.' Petod places the money in the sliding tray.

The man pulls it in, looks marginally happier and drops a key stick in the tray to slide it out. 'Room 26, second floor.' He gestures to stairs at the back of the foyer. They climb dusty spaces lit by the sugar-bag bodies of luminescent aphids clinging to a half dead light vine, enter a corridor and, counting out the numbers, find their apartment. Petod inserts the key stick in the slot beside the oval door, which clicks open. As they enter he inserts it in the activation portal and the lights come on. Two sofas lounge in the first room, detachable soft screens are scattered and a wall screen painted. In a kitchen area off to one side he abandons bags of comestibles. Doors open into two bedrooms each with en suite. He has never stayed somewhere so luxurious before. He walks over to two large upright oval windows. One is fixed but the other opens as a door onto a metal grid balcony rimmed with overflowing plant pots. A flight of bats flaps away above.

'This will do?' he asks.

She shrugs. 'Of course.'

In the night whose light is no different from the day, Petod wakes. Sensing a presence in his room, momentary terror assails him. A fist to the control on the bedpost ignites star lights in the ceiling, revealing the figure just inside the door.

After a moment, he manages. 'You could not sleep.'

Yoon is wearing only knickers and the short top she wore under her city clothing. Though he has seen her naked the sight is now intensely erotic. Her nipples jut against the material and with her right hand she is stroking her stomach. A smell, musky, permeates the air and seems to leech into his skin and head, to make a path directly to his genitals. He feels embarrassed by the immediate physical reaction, because of the attack upon her, and how he must not see her as he now sees her.

'Sleep is only a matter of choice for me,' she tells him, and walks round to stand beside the bed. She reaches down and gently takes hold of the blanket. She pulls at it but he holds on, trying to find a route through his sudden confusion.

'You were raped,' he manages.

'It was violence, assault, and this is not.'

His will breaks and he releases the blanket. She pulls it back, exposing his naked body and complete readiness.

'You have a good body,' she says, 'considering the mix that made you.' She steps back and pulls off the top, then slides her knickers down to her ankles and steps out of them. 'But do you have control?'

He is mute until she closes a hand around his penis. He groans and tenses his buttocks. Yes, he damned well has control. He can last for as long as he chooses and ride the waves of pleasure to exhaustion, while his refractory period is short enough to continue play until the next wave. Even so, when she squats down and slides her mouth over his penis and begins tickling the base of his glans with her tongue he nearly comes. The feelings have never been so intense before and he knows her pheromones and the sheer reality of her are affecting him on many levels. She plays with him for a time, slowly working down until he is deep in her throat, then withdraws. He panics thinking she is now just going to walk away, but she moves to the base of the bed and grabs his ankles to drag him further down. The ease with which she does this tells him something of her strength.

Next she climbs onto the bed and up beside him, straddles his chest with her back to him, slides her arse up to his face and offers a wet slot, before going down on his penis again. He kisses the lips, loving the pure taste of sex, runs his tongue around her anus then laps at her like a dog at a water bowl. He inserts his tongue, frees an arm and works in a finger too. She groans and rides his face, rubs his penis with one hand while licking and sucking the head. She shudders, pressing hard down on his face and grinding, very wet now. He keeps working her and struggles to retain control. She comes again, and then a third time. It then becomes too much and he thrusts up into her mouth and lets it go, yelling as he does so. The pleasure passes through him in a wave as of a drug and momentary dizziness assails him.

Yoon dismounts, turns round and slides up beside him. Her elbow on the bed and head on her hand she studies his face, reaches out with her other hand to wipe the fluid from it and inserts a finger in her mouth.

'We have only just begun,' she says.

'You have to give me some time,' he replies.

'Really?' she asks, sliding a hand down his body to grasp his flaccid cock.

'Yes, really, I need. . .' He cannot believe it because he is rising again. In a small and still functional part of his mind he knows she is asserting control over him that goes beyond mere touch, but he does not care. He is ready. He pushes himself up, grabs her and drags her below him. She fights him but without the strength he knows she has. This bothers him, considering what has brought them here, but his control is sliding away. He forces her legs open and she claws his back and though he feels actual damage, even that is pleasure. He sinks into her, and into hours where his intellect shrinks to a minuscule point.

Yoon rises out of sleep she does not require but has indulged through convention. Petod sleeps on in exhaustion and she knows he is not yet even capable of waking. Pain and pleasure flow around each other in her mind like immiscible fluids. The mixture is unhealthy but she acknowledges her need to have asserted dominance over at least this man.

She climbs out of the bed, picks up her underwear and heads to her room, where she showers and dresses, and then out into the main room of the apartment. It is day out in the world, but no concession to that down here, for the lighting outside is unchanged. Adjusted to the shadow, she does not turn on lights as she goes in the kitchen area where she makes coffee whose flavour she had forgotten until last night. She drinks and lounges on a sofa. An hour passes, perhaps two. She makes another coffee, now hearing Petod moving about, taking a shower, smiles and stands. He is hers now, utterly. She walks out onto the steel balcony and with all her senses studies the plants, taking in their chemical output. They are highly adjusted to survive in the meagre light from street lamps, and from the faded sun globes in the tangled roof of this place. She finds an old chair of wood toughened with the organic metal wires of its initial growth, and sits.

This place is much changed since last she was here, but also, so much is the same. The humans strive for the same concerns and have the same needs as before, just dressed up in different clothes. Power, love, sex and survival are all as they have always been. She reaches out now to the Bosch but can only catch a brief sense of them. Hidden and skulking in shadow they seek the scents of their respective fathers. She sips coffee and waits, knowing one will soon enough find a trail. Then something new draws her attention: shouting from below. She stands and moves to the edge of the balcony to peer down. Four policemen are beating someone on the ground. Finally satisfied their victim is either unconscious or dead, they turn to the door of a tenement block and go inside.

'They're searching the city for you,' says Petod, walking out with his own beaker of coffee.

Now studying his expression she sees a lost look – one almost of betrayal. Yes, he is hers, but he also understands she has chemically bound him. She questions her impulse last night and feels shame. His reaction to her actions at the station affected her like this too, so did she bind him because of that *criticism*?

'Why?' She belatedly registers his comment, realizing he has checked public feeds while in his room.

'You committed an assault against the mayor and city officials. It's a loss of face they cannot countenance.'

She gazes at him steadily. 'I should perhaps have been more diplomatic.'

'Perhaps.' He moves over to look down into the street. 'But their search is, coincidentally, of those places under gang control and so not paying the mayoral levy. It's just an excuse to . . . stir things a little.'

She nods and moves back into the apartment, hungry now and needing to prepare, for now she has touched the mind of one of her creatures. He follows her inside, grimacing at the link that draws him in her wake. Rather than eat the raw and fresh things he bought in the supermarket, this time she eats sweet bread and preserved meat. She is swallowing the last mouthful when she senses the approach above and, shortly afterwards, hears a shout of panic and slamming doors.

'I don't think they're in this building.' Petod is puzzled, referring to the police.

A shadow occludes the glass and shortly afterwards comes a harsh tap tapping. Petod, his back to the balcony, freezes momentarily then shrugs and puts down the remains of his sandwich, fighting the fear that has winged in.

'It's one of them, isn't it?'

'Open the door,' she instructs.

He stands, turns and heads over, trying not to see what is outside as he opens the door. The Bird ducks in and moves past him, briefly eyeing him and flicking out a sharp tongue, its musky stale odour filling the place. She senses it absolutely now: its eagerness for completion. The scent trail is its father's. The others are still following that but it has returned for her, as is the way, so she can observe the final act. Petod heads to his room to get ready, acknowledging by his actions what he only knows unconsciously. Yoon collects her Cougar handgun and concealing cape. The Bird moves out onto the balcony and takes flight with a whoomph of great wings, sailing up into the rafters. Yoon and Petod descend vined exterior stairs to the street. Her connection remains firm as the Bird launches again winging along above, and they follow on foot below.

'It's found them?' Petod finally manages.

'Just the one,' she replies.

At the end of the street they climb a spiral stair marked by one greasy feather. Further streets ensue, and alleys where the Bird looms to send people shrieking and fleeing. Soon they come to where semi-automated industry blocks and warehouses sit under open sky. The Bird takes to the air again, drifts across like a giant vulture to come down in a flurry of feathers before the entrance into a factory. Sounds of mechanical movement issue from within, as of a hive of giant metal bees. The Bird stalks through into the oily racketing darkness.

They follow the creature to where machine arms shift and conveyors convey, while techs in long white leather observe shifting displays. Unrecognisable engine components drop smoking from moulds and others hammer form under presses overseen by techs in enclosed booths, thick goggles blackening their eyes. A lathe screams, ejecting a ribbon of swarf that could cut a man in half, coolant sprays and hisses. Yoon feels such old industry is a sign of decline.

While the Bird moves on, the Plague Doctor waits in the greasy shadow of some looming machine. It waves a claw for them to follow as it slides out. A man in a rubber apron rounds the machine and sees it face on. He holds up hands in thick gloves and closes his eyes, expecting an end, but it simply moves round him. As they skulk through the shifting machine-scape, Yoon sees workers and techs gathering and closing in. Some are drawn by her presence, some by curiosity, while a few pick up tools perhaps for violence or defence. Sparks rain down, perhaps from some ancient welder. Yoon looks up as Petod grabs her arm and drags her to cover. No, not a welder. Someone has just taken a shot at them.

'Up there.' He points up to a figure fleeing along a gantry. She gestures to the Plague Doctor and it moves away. She senses Catape and Cowfish close too, but cannot see them.

They reach a stair, the Doctor flowing up ahead, and climb. People in clean city wear goggle from behind windows comprised of hexagonal crystals, some rising from desks. The gantry shakes as she steps out onto it – others mounting the stair below. Ahead, shadow slides through a door, briefly revealing a white carp head glancing back at her. As the Doctor goes through next, shots ring out, throwing burning metal from the jamb. She crouches beside the door checking her weapon, but does not want it to be necessary. Petod has drawn a gun too. She sees he has brought an antique slammer. Good – it does not kill. Abruptly she throws herself through the door, taking in her surroundings in a glance, then scrambling behind a stack of crates. Petod comes through next to hide behind a smaller stack, which begins exploding into splinters. He scrabbles away from that behind a metal mantis loading machine.

'Come on you fuckers!'

The Batian stands on a large fluid tank, backed up against pipework running up towards the ceiling. The Cowfish obliges, sliding into view and rolling across intervening floor. He pumps his weapon and fires a grenade. The blast opens out the Cowfish like a great mass of sheets, and sends it tumbling and burning. It begins to collapse together again and reconstitute as another shadow flees it, arriving below the tank. The Catape climbs, digging claws into the metalwork. The man above shoulders the strap of his weapon and climbs too – looking for handholds on the mass of pipes. He ascends fast, but not fast enough to avoid the Catape's claw around his ankle. Drawing a sidearm he shoots down at it, just as the ibis head of the Plague Doctor peers around from the other side of the pipes. He shrieks, loses grip, as the Bird swoops down on him and the Doctor flows round. Wrapped in shadow and the terrible embraces of the Bosch, he falls screaming, but slow as a dandelion seed. Yoon stands and steps out from cover, lesions in her mind twisting together like threads and shrinking, but one opening out wide. A moment later Petod follows and they advance towards frenetic shadow difficult to encompass, but which spills the Batian's weapons, and then his armour and his clothing.

'Maybe more trouble,' says Petod, looking back.

Yoon glances round, seeing the factory inhabitants crowding through doors and walking out onto gantries in this place. She makes an effort to think – to step out of the process. Yes, some hold makeshift weapons but she understands these are more for comfort than intent. These people are as much here to witness as is she. With Petod dogging her footsteps, then pulling back at the last, she steps into the Bosch shadows and they clear around her. The Batian is naked on his knees and now she recognizes him. A portion of memory begins to open ready to shed it load of pain. He struggles but the Plague Doctor's grip is firm, claws digging into the flesh below his shoulders.

. . . the Batian looms into sight. He has stripped down to a padded undersuit. Holding a cylinder to his nose he sniffs and his eyes start shivering in his skull. A moment later he is kneeling between her legs and freeing his erect penis. He leans forwards and punches her hard in the face but this does not distract her from giving the

internal instruction and making herself wet. He drives in, determined to hurt, grabs her throat and chokes her as he pumps at her. Finally he comes and she feels the wet warmth flowing inside.

Do they know? *She wonders. . .*

The intensity of it hurts and then begins to fade as it incorporates with the full extent of her mind. Emotions lock as she segues into practicality.

'Where are the others?' she asks him.

He is shaking his head and squirming, caught in a fever dream, seemingly dragged into a supernatural world in a milieu that has long dismissed that idea. Finally he focuses on her.

'Fuck you,' he says, inevitably.

'Where are they?'

'Far away and over the hills,' he mutters.

'You will die,' she says, not prepared to lie by adding, 'If you don't tell me.'

'I don't know.'

'Why did Ibruk want you to do what you did?'

He just stares and she realizes she is procrastinating, because that answer he knows was given just before this man raped her. Further delay will gain no answers. She looks around. Witnesses, with Petod among them, have drawn closer, the scene now visible through the shadow. The Cowfish has drawn itself together. It will need to feed for full strength, but is ready to move again. Looking to the Bird she raises her hand and affirms with a gesture the instruction she sends directly to its mind. It has grown now and looms ten feet tall, bloated and loose. It heron steps forwards with its greasy wings spread, and opens its toothed beak wide, looming over the man as the Plague Doctor releases him. He gazes up into its wet maw and crazy revolving eyes and sees his future, and screams as it lungs down like a stork on a frog. It raises him high, shoulder and torso in its beak, legs kicking, arms flailing. It crunches and mauls him until his head is pointing down its throat, blood spattering and a loop of intestine dropping from a split. His screams grow muffled as it begins to swallow, then turn to weird groans through its neck as he slides inside. He is still kicking when only his feet can be seen and its neck bulges. Then swallowed at last he fights inside like a rabbit in a sack. He must have an anoxia adaptation, for it takes him a long time to die. And as he dies that lesion in her mind closes down to a thread.

Many of the crowd are now down on their knees, while Petod has covered his face with his hands. She nods, for this is as it should be, and walks over to stand before the Bird. It sinks down, its body shrinking to the tune of crunching bone. It bows its head – a hunger now satisfied in the only way possible. She rests a hand on that head – permission granted. The Bird shudders and collapses further, splits opening in its body and spilling putrid internal organs, feathers dropping away. Pieces of the man fall out too, for he has been broken apart in the same accelerated decay. The whole mass sinks and settles, vile juices spreading across the floor, a foul vapour rising. Eventually there is nothing left but a great pool of organic decay.

'You have reached completion,' says Yoon.

The streets stink of fear. People rush about their business and head home as quickly afterwards. Four days have passed since the events in the factory, but the Bosch, though finding scent trails, have followed them to dead ends. The other two Batians, the Krodorman and the albino woman, have disappeared. Two days have now passed since Yoon made her demand through the city media, but the police, no matter how many doors kicked in or suspects beaten, have found no sign of her attackers. Yesterday, a protest at the mayor's offices, driven by terror of roaming Bosch, turned into a riot. None of this has been directly helpful. The city officials and the police are inept but, as he opined when he suggested she make her demand, it has put pressure on others. Sieving through reports and paying where necessary, he has at last found a name.

Petod walks into the bar, sees the man drinking alone, a soft screen stuck on the table before him. He walks over, noting three rough boardapts – huge men with piggish heads and tusks – observing him. Fender likes to drink alone, but Fender always stays protected. Standing at the table, he notes how it grows darker in here, and that others have arrived. One of the boardapts sees, with confusion, a tall cloaked figure stooped over the bar next to him. The barman serves a drink, eyes wide and staring beyond the figure, his subconscious forcing his rational mind to ignore what is in front of him.

'What do you want?' Fender looks up.

Petod pulls out a chair and sits. He would never have been so brave before. The boardapts shift hands to bulges in their clothing, grunt preparation for violence.

'I need to know the location of the people Yoon is seeking,' he says.

'Oh really?'

'I am prepared to pay one hundred thousand a head for the Batians and two-hundred-and-fifty thousand each for the other two.'

Fender puts his elbows on the table, makes a cage of his fingers and rests his chin on them. He sits there for a long time observing Petod.

'You're from the mayor's office?' he enquires, but the question seems insincere.

'No.'

'Private contractor?'

'Yes.'

'I see,' says Fender. 'Leave now and you get to stay alive.'

'You're saying you don't know where they are? My information says otherwise.'

'Your information is wrong. And now you have tried my patience to the limit.'

He sits back and snaps his fingers. One of the boardapts begins to move away from the bar towards their table, but the large figure beside him turns, stoops and comes up again. The movements are difficult to track, but the effect is easy to see. The big heavy man, jerks up, leaves the floor and hurtles across the room with arms windmilling. He crashes into the street window of the bar, shattering many of the numerous small panes but fails to break their composite frame, and crashes down onto a table, collapsing it.

Another of the heavies begins shrieking and squealing, staggering across the room seemingly surrounded by shifting shadow containing hints of fur, claws and teeth. The place grows darker and the squealing recedes. Heavy weights thump against the floor. A yell, and another crash. More squealing and the sound of someone running through rooms and crashing through door. Squealing turns to whimpering in the darkness, then terminates with a horrible wet swallowing sound. Petod looks around. It is as if the place has slid into another dimension – a darker place, a Hellish place. Out of the shadows to one side the Cowfish looms and tastes the air with its octopus tongue. Petod studies it for a moment.

'One of your men is gone,' he says. 'The others may recover.'

'Gone?' Fender inquires, and Petod admires his apparent calm.

He gestures to the Cowfish. 'It needed to feed and, since your bodyguards are multiply guilty of murder.' He shrugs.

Fender is facing straight forwards then, as if his neck is corroded by age, he slowly turns his head to look at the creature looming by the table.

'I never believed, even when there were pictures,' he says. 'I suppose that's because what is simply biology is now perceived as something supernatural, and I can never believe in that.'

Yoon now steps out of the shadows, walks over and pulls out a chair. She turns it and sits astride it.

'Allow me to introduce –'

'I know who she is,' Fender interrupts, turning towards her. 'Seems I am in a bad situation and must renege on promises made and services provided.'

Petod notes something in the tone and does not like it.

'You must tell me where they are,' says Yoon.

Fender spreads his hands, accepting this apparently bad situation. 'The two you put the higher price on . . . I cannot tell you where they are. I helped them all disappear as per their instructions, which I now see entailed breaking some kind of trail.' He studies Yoon for a moment. 'A scent trail? Are they like bloodhounds?'

She nods agreement and he continues, 'Those two properly disappeared. But the two Batians are rather more careless – employing urchins to buy the things they need and who, as you may know, also like to sell information.'

'Where are they?' Yoon asks.

He begins to reach into his pocket and in response the Cowfish surges closer.

'May I?' he asks.

At Yoon's nod he extracts an antique notebook and pen. In decorous cursive script he writes down an address, carefully detaches the leaf of paper and slides it across to her. She picks it up, studies it briefly and inserts it in her pocket.

'I now have to decide if you are lying about the other two and whether it will be necessary to use persuasion,' she says.

'What can I say to convince you?' Fender asks and, for the first time, Petod sees real fear in his expression. 'I know you're real now.' He gestures to the Cowfish. 'And that they are too. I would be a fool to lie now.'

'Very well.' She stands, gestures to her pocket. 'If this turns out to be correct I will move money into your account. If not. . .'

Fender gestures to his surroundings. 'You know where to find me.'

As they depart, the shadows flowing out of the bar and scattering to the darker portions of the street around them, Petod feels something is wrong.

'We must have a care,' he says. 'That all seemed too easy.'

'I know,' Yoon replies.

The apartment blocks built against the inner face of the city wall are constructed one atop another like columns of haphazardly stacked books. Closely crowded buildings opposite delimit a street resembling a canyon, within which an open air market has been sited. Yoon studies the blocks as they walk, counting in from the one nearest the gate tower. Having tuned down her pheromone output, people here only stare at her in curiosity, puzzled as to why. She and Petod are nearly to the sixth block when Catape's eagerness is a flurry of shadowy movement flitting between stalls then disappearing into an alley between looming edifices. The trail is fresh – only minutes old.

'Come on!' She hurries after the creature.

Petod runs beside her as other shadows enter the alley ahead. She glances round, seeing the people now converging. The excitement of the chase has ramped up her output and now those who are hers, or partially hers, begin to really notice of her. A shriek issues from ahead when they are deep into the alleyway. They follow it to a small square where stone mermaids vomit water into a surrounding pool of water lilies. A man staggers past in the opposite direction, terrified, trying to close a case spilling drug bulbs and packets. She knows, in an instant, why the Batian has strayed from cover – the remembered smell of addiction on skin during the act of rape.

By the fountain, a bulky figure fights shadow. A sawing beam of energy stabs out flaking stone from one mermaid. It stabs again lifting cobblestones like hot fish scales. The figure crashes down as the Catape tears at him, stripping away the heavy atmosphere suit he wore to conceal his scent. The weapon flames again, cutting up through the body of the Catape just as the other two Bosch arrive. The Ape knocks the weapon away, hissing smoke from its mouth. As the shadows close round, the Plague Doctor looming up for a moment, impossibly tall, Petod picks up the weapon and turns to her. She nods acknowledgement and moves into the shadow.

This Batian is a real scrapper and this is appropriate really, since he fathered the Catape. The Doctor and the Cowfish hold back as the Batian and Catape brawl – the man wielding a curved knife, then plucked away and discarded. Soon the Ape denudes him of his suit and attacks his inner clothing. Both leak blood, though the Ape's is yellow like pus. Finally the man can fight no more and, bleeding and naked, crawls along the ground to the edge of the fountain, while the Catape tracks along behind him, licking its wounds. The Plague Doctor now strides in to flip the man over and push him back against the fountain wall. Yoon steps closer and looks down at him.

The memory this time is of fevered speculation after the last raped her. In the cave she was aware that for every attack on her people a price is exacted – some form of biological revenge. The thought is incomplete and without language as her new attacker comes. Pain memory arises for this man has a penis ribbed with keratin and no amount of moisture stopped the damage and he stepped away from her bloody. Logic ensues and now with the mind for it her speculation continues. They did not attack one of her people but *her* and the price therefore is consequently high and certain. Was it coincidence that they found her out of the millions of those who live on her world?

'Where are Ibruk and the albino woman?' she asks.

He smiles crazily up at her and opens his mouth to reveal a packet of white powder, already spilling its contents. The Doctor snaps a claw down to catch his jaw, but it is already too late for he bites and chews. He groans, face twisting in ecstasy, and then his back arches, his eyes rolling up in his head. There will be no answers here. She gestures to the Catape to affirm her mental signal, and the creature leaps on him.

The Catape tears at him in a frenzy, stripping flesh from bone, opening his torso and strewing viscera, but every blow, every injury simply makes the man writhe with pleasure. The Ape shrieks its objection to this road to completion. With the man eviscerated yet still clinging to life, it hauls him up and over the low wall into the lily pool and shoves him under, where perhaps drowning is a pleasure too. Eventually it is done and the Catape sits up to its chest in bloody water. This time Yoon does not touch to give permission, simply nods. The Ape sinks into the pool, the water bubbling around it, lily pads curl and turn yellow. It is out of sight for a minute when objects begin floating to the surface: here a mass of fur attached to slimy skin, there the stripped skull of the Batian. The stink rises as a green smoke and soon liquefying body parts scum the whole pool. The Catape rises up for a moment, skeleton intact yet all but bare of flesh, then that too falls apart as it collapses back down again.

'The other one,' says Yoon, turning away, bitter with the Catape's dissatisfaction and her own feeling that the attack on her had not been as simple as she thought.

The people witness and Petod's expression is one of inured horror. She walks through the crowd, some reaching out to touch her, but losing their nerve at the last. Petod follows, trying to catch up but failing in the press. Out in the market she feels a surge of rage and instructs the Bosch. They move through the crowd shoving people aside and issuing chemical terror. At once people are screaming, crying and fighting to get away. They clear around her leaving Petod alone – already immunized to this. He comes up beside her.

'None of this feels right to me,' he says.

'Then leave,' she replies.

'I cannot.'

She crosses the market, the Bosch moving quickly ahead on the back trail of the man the Catape just killed. They mount a stair zigging and zagging up the side of an apartment block. Five apartments up they arrive at a studded and armoured door. She gestures them aside and points her Cougar at one side of it and fires, but the beads, though exploding with viciousness that drives her and Petod back to the stair, just create glowing dents. The weapon is too dangerous for this task, she decides.

'Let me try.' The Batain weapon burns deep around the lock like a thermic lance. After a moment he kicks the door, but it does not budge. He burns away the rest of the lock and is about to try again when the Plague Doctor moves in his way, reaches a claw through the red hot hole and heaves. The door tears away with a high, almost female shriek, and the creature tosses it down the stairs. Yoon feels a moment of disquiet. She knows the durability of this kind of door and realizes this version of the Doctor is uncommonly strong. Something about the genetic addition from its father perhaps, or an errant mutation?

She and Petod follow as the two remaining Bosch enter strewing shadow and confusion around them. Luxuries abound here with sofas recessed in a gemstone floor. Computer links include a virtual sphere, while the kitchen is automated. She expects gunfire again, but the man by the wide window, thought armed, does not open fire on them.

'So you are here,' he says bitterly. 'Velch was a fool. I told him that suit wouldn't work, that the atmosphere seals were too old.'

The apartment continues to darken, and becomes a world encysted in shadow, the Bosch only half-seen presences. She recognizes the man as the one, beside the albino, who caused her the most pain. His rape ensuing on that of his damaging fellow, he could not cum until he had bitten one of her breasts so hard he had nearly detached a nipple.

'Where are Ibruk and the albino?' she asks.

'And if I tell you?'

She just stares at him, desperate for information but unable to promise him his life. She holds up a hand, stilling the two Bosch and studies the scene. This man must have been aware of the uproar below, yet has not fled. He is in full armour, with its shock absorbing facility, and he is over by the window. Her thought goes out and the Bosch comply – the Plague Doctor weaving further shadow and spreading murk to cover the Cowfish's retreat.

'You die quickly,' she finally says.

'Oh wonderful. How nice for me.'

'Why did you do what you did?'

'Because I was paid.'

'Why did Ibruk pay you to do this?'

'Why why why? Are you a child?'

She studies him again. His life is just a blink of time to her and he calls her child. He seeks to distract. The resources available to a man trained in arts martial give rise to possibilities. Her thought goes out to the doctor. It will have to be fast and, of course, the Batian already knows the fastest route. The Doctor expands itself, insinuating out into shadow, tightening sinews and charging muscle.

'I have not been a child in a very long time,' she says, glancing over to Petod. Can he survive this? She thinks he can, but he needs to be closer. 'Petod, come over to my side.' He looks puzzled but complies. 'Now stay by my side.' She begins to walk forwards scanning about herself. It could be anywhere in here, but there is no advantage to her finding it.

The Batian's watchfulness betrays that he is marking their position in the room. Just a slight change in his features and she knows.

'Far enough,' he says, and shoots out the window behind him.

Now, she tells the Plague Doctor.

Her senses accelerate, slowing the procession of events. The Batian turns to the window as the Doctor folds in out of shadow, embracing both herself and Petod in greased darkness, a claw folding around her waist and another around his, fungus robes and expanded body closing up. The Batian jumps – his armour sufficient for him to survive the fall. The Doctor springs forwards, taut muscle burning sugar and oxygen in a flare of energy. Its acceleration towards the window cracks her joints and jounces air from her lungs. Behind, the explosive device in the apartment detonates, a wave of fire pursuing them. They go over the edge, the Batian falling ahead, feet downwards. The blast from the apartment window clips them, burning fabric and flesh peeling from the Doctor. They tumble in flapping sheets of darkness, then slow to the descent of a pricked balloon. Below the Batian hits the ground and rolls, suit joints jetting steam cooling. He comes up between stalls but it seems a shadowy place in the market. He turns to look back as the Cowfish surges out of nowhere and bites down on him, taking his head and upper body into its maw.

The Plague doctor hits and unravels, spilling them on the ground. She goes down on her hands and knees and looks across at Petod. The man is not moving

55

and she can sense injury, but his breath and heartbeat are still strong. The Batian shrieks as the Cowfish tries and fails to crunch his armour. As she rises she gives consent and it takes him down armour and all.

Her joints creaking, she internally accelerates repairs, and walks over to Petod. Reaching down she touches his chest, then parting his shirt gently presses in her claws to read him. He is unconscious, ribs and other bones cracked – the radius in his forearm broken. Internally she tailors a package for him and injects it – maintaining his unconsciousness and speeding healing, sending specially-loaded vesicles to his skull to search out and stop the potential for a haematoma.

When done she turns back to see the Cowfish experiencing problems. She walks closer as the man inside the creature fights to survive – the air supply of his suit keeping him alive. It must be the armour blocking the Cowfish. Closer still she reaches out, pushing claws into pallid flesh. No, it has penetrated his armour and sent in its connections to its father, ready to integrate them both in dual accelerated decay, but the feedback is all wrong, as if the man inside is not its intended victim. The Cowfish begins shivering and she steps back, baffled. It heaves and shudders and then in a great flood of bile shot through with the connection fibres, vomits him out onto the ground. It howls then in frustration and pain.

Yoon steps over to the man to peer down at him. He is still alive and crawls out of the flood, turns over and looks up at her. He opens his suit mask.

'You are not the father of my child,' she says.

He gazes at her puzzled for a moment, then glances to the Cowfish.

'So it's true,' he says.

'Why are you not the father?'

He focuses on her again. 'Let me live and I will tell you why.'

She finds room for manoeuvre in her driving purpose – her method. It is actually possible for her to step back and not be the final arbiter of his fate.

'I will let you live if you also tell me where the other two are,' she states, and casts her thought to her two remaining Bosch.

'I am told that you do not lie and your word is adamantine,' he says. He heaves himself up into a sitting position. 'I had time to prepare for Ibruk's chore when the others did not, or did not care to. We were to rape you and, though I did not believe all Ibruk said, I was not so foolish as to spill my own seed in you since it could be traced to me.'

'So what did you do?'

'I raped you with another man's balls.'

She is suddenly curious about this. 'And your own?'

'In storage should I want them back. I don't plan on fathering—' He pauses and looks at the Cowfish again, then spits out, 'children.'

She nods. 'Now tell me the location of Ibruk and the albino.'

He stands, unsteadily, blood leaking through gaps in his armour. 'You'll find him tucked away in the Embassy, heavily defended. I don't know if even your creatures can get to him there.'

'Thank you,' she says, and turns away.

A stall crashes aside because from the free will she has granted the Plague Doctor it has made its decision. The Cowfish, free to make its own decisions too, does not move. It is wounded inside by the failed completion and now little inclined to violence. Behind her she hears the man's, 'You promised!' and then his shriek of pain. Something bloody and clad in armour thumps down to one side as she goes back to Petod and squats beside him.

Petod dreams that shadows carry him, their cold bloody claws around him. He slides through the under-city and hears the creak of iron steps, sees vines threading through darkness. Chemical terror waxes and wanes, bats flit above ill-lit foamstone that is clad in blue lichen. Now softness engulfs him and he feels cold and wet wrap over the pain in his arm while it seems a fever of microscopic bees hum busily inside him. And then he opens his eyes.

He is in his bed in the apartment they rented. His body feels sticky and hot and aches and, pushing back the blanket, he sees a biocast moulded around his forearm. Only a moment later does he turn and see Yoon sitting in a chair beside the bed, wrapped in a large towel.

'What . . . happened?' he manages.

'The Batian mined his apartment intending to kill us. The Plague Doctor got us out, but it was rough. Your injuries are near healed, however.'

'Did they get him?'

'Yes.' She stands and walks over beside the bed. Instantly he is reminded of the last time this happened and, despite his aches feels a similar reaction to before.

'How did I get here?' he asks, trying to delay what he knows his coming.

'The Plague Doctor carried you.'

Shuddering at the half memory of cold claws around him he asks, 'So now we must search again for the other two? Perhaps they got away somehow – off-world?'

He hopes so and that this is the end of it. Her presence compels him and he cannot just walk away from her as she suggested, but her actions horrify him. On a deep level he feels anger at her attackers and sees the punishment of their crime as necessary. But must the punishments be so grotesque? Do her attackers need to die when they did not commit murder? Yet he knows that the Batians, for it is their trade, and probably those who employed them, must be guilty of taking lives.

She presses a hand down on the bed, staring at him, then pulls the blanket down and sits astride him, to begin rubbing herself against his belly. He has a sudden horrible thought. What if she is holding his seed inside her and intends to make something with it, something like the Bosch? He half expects the thought to kill his erection. It does not, especially when she casts the towel aside. She then stops moving.

'I know where they are,' she finally says, and starts moving again.

'How?'

She grimaces. 'The Batian told me.' There is something else she is not telling, but her grinding hips blow the thought out of his mind.

'Where are they?' he manages.

'Not yet – we have something else to do right now.' She lifts up and slides back.

'I don't know if I can,' he says.

'You can.' She reaches between her legs and guides him inside her.

This time she orgasms once, then tells him to let go. He does, arching his back as if trying to reach her heart, emptying and emptying until it seems his balls are clenching dry. She dismounts and steps off the bed.

'Remove that cast and ready yourself,'

She leaves, picking up her towel on the way. Petod feels calmer now – the oldest cure having worked for him. He lies there gathering further calm, then sits upright and studies the cast. This biotech made here on this world is red when applied and now, with the bone healed underneath it has changed to a dull blue. He pulls off a tag at the top and the thing softens. An inserted finger opens out a developing split and he peels it away exposing an interior like the underside of a starfish. His skin is red from nano-needle punctures but that will soon fade.

Petod showers and dresses, places his slammer back in the belt loop underneath is jacket then dons his city cape over that – shimmer mask in a pocket. In the main room of the apartment Yoon is dressed, now in an insulated body suit, the Cougar at her hip again. The place is well lit and no shadows lurk inside or out on the balcony.

'Where is the Doctor?' he asks.

'With the Cowfish down by the Embassy

'I thought they died when they found and killed their fathers. Why is the Cowfish still alive? Did you release that Batian in exchange for information?'

'His genetics were not those in his seed, therefore the Cowfish could not reach completion. In exchange for information I promised not to kill him.'

'I am surprised – I did not think you capable of . . . bargaining.'

She stared at him. 'The Plague Doctor, of its own volition, killed him.'

He nods, uncomfortable now with this capability for half-truths.

'The Embassy?' he asks.

'Where Ibruk and the albino woman are hiding,' she replies.

'The Embassy,' he repeats dully. As a grant of land simply for habitation, the city comes under her jurisdiction. The Embassy, built on land passed in perpetuity to a conglomerate of off-world polities, is jurisdictionally as the name implies. Under her own agreements she has no legal power there for it is not her territory. 'You can't just go in there and do what you want.'

She turns to him. 'Most of the concerns there have free movement of citizens between and through their territories and that applies to the Embassy too. I am free to go into that place if I so wish. But yes, there are limitations on what *I* can do there.'

He notes the emphasis, considers how the Plague Doctor killed that man of *its own volition* and sees her intent. By law a killers on Embassy territory must forfeit their own lives. He can see how the court will know precisely the motivator of the killing, but will conveniently ignore that. Not that it would even get to a court. He thinks it highly unlikely anyone there will try to arrest the ruler of a world who is also the world itself.

She heads out onto the balcony. He hesitates, thinking about turning to the apartment door and heading away. Just the thought raises a deep anxiety at the prospect of separation, and he follows her out. She has bound him, and he knows she did it during sex the first time, for the feeling was not so strong before that. No doubt this last time she climbed on him to reinforce the bond. He feels bitter and struggles to hold onto that, but it is gone by the time they reach the street.

'You lead the way,' she says.

Moving ahead he thinks about where they are. The quickest way to the Embassy is through the low tunnels. He gestures and leads the way to the nearest stair and they spiral down into gloom. He has chosen this quickest route because he wants resolution. Will she free him after she has achieved her goals? Even that thought makes him anxious. As much as he wants his freedom he does not, and cannot want freedom from her at the moment. Only his intellect recognizes the utterly chemical source of his feelings, but is all but swamped by them.

Faintly luminescent tiles, whose sum output is enough to see by, line the low tunnels. He walks in the general direction of the Embassy until reaching an intersection and reading the sign there writ in an old runic script. Now knowing the way he takes a turning, stepping with care not to crush the side spiral snails, and crawling gnapper bugs. Glowing veins, like capillaries but bright blue, complement the light. It is deposited by the gnappers and so considered a faux pas to kill them. The snails he avoids because he hates the crunch of life extinguished and knows from experience their slipperiness can put him on his face.

They take three turnings before reaching the upward stair, and climb ten spirals to a studded compressed fibre door. Glancing up he sees camera nodules above no doubt linked to the Embassy, and curses for not thinking to have them both don their shimmer masks. Perhaps a watcher will not recognize them, though he suspects an alert in that place for Yoon. He pushes up the palm lock and opens the door with an ornate handle fashioned in the shape of a snake. Daylight blinds him for a moment, but as Yoon steps out beside him his vision returns. They stand in a wide square with roads around it and others starring off into numerous streets. This part of the city remains open enough for cars. In the square's centre is the statue garden with its flower borders, fountains and, of course, statues. One at the centre is a precise but enlarged depiction of the woman beside him.

'I can feel them close.' She points. 'They are in the garden, waiting.' She turns towards the Embassy.

They see just one outer face of an octagonal building five floors tall. Barred windows face out, while a pillared portico leads to the public entrance. The security is inside and he wonders how it will react.

Yoon leads the way along the pavement, pauses at a road to watch a hover tram slide past, then crosses.

They pass many shops here selling expensive clothing, shoes and scents. Yoon pauses by one packed with planetary biologicals.

'My people need to come here and look very carefully at these prices,' she opines, then moves on.

The comment is too prosaic to register with him, when he knows that murder is imminent. Finally they mount the steps to the portico and head towards open doors.

Yoon pauses on the threshold to peer in at the carpeted foyer, the scanning arch and armed security guards Clad in Batian armour. Perhaps they are Batians – she does not know. Turning she gazes out at the park to send her summons. Shadow slips between statues, disrupts the spray of a fountain, but the Bosch cannot maintain their disguise in full daylight as they move to the kerb on the far side of the road. A woman screams, drops packages and runs. A hover transport mounts the pavement and ploughs into a lamp post. The two Bosch patiently watch a car slow as it passes them, then cross the road. Yoon nods, and steps into the Embassy.

With Petod beside her she strides to the security arch, studies it for a moment, then unholsters her weapon. Security guards on the other side raise short stubby carbines and watch as she places the weapon on a tray beside the arch. A cover snaps over it, drawing it from sight, then extrudes empty again and opens its cover. Petod takes out his slammer, places it on the tray too, and it too is similarly taken. He walks through the arch first and it green-lights him. As Yoon steps through, multiple lights ignite all over the thing, skittering here and there. On the other side a guard approaches, holding out a scanner – two others at her back – meanwhile a plaintive alarm sounds inside the Embassy.

'What other items do you have?' asks the woman.

'None,' Yoon replies.

'What enhancements?'

'Only what I am.'

'Sparic! Look at this!' says another guard.

The woman with the scanner turns towards the arch and her mouth drops open. The Plague Doctor comes through fast, the arch screeing strangely and its lights going crazy. Cowfish elicits a similar reaction. The woman holds up her hand scanner and looks askance at it.

'Welcome! Welcome Yoon!' cries a short but wide heavyworlder clad in businesswear – obviously one of the Embassy officials. Yoon eyes him. Yet again she has no time for this, because the Doctor now has the trail of Ibruk.

'I am going inside to see someone,' she says to the guards. 'I suggest you don't try to stop me.' The Plague Doctor breaks into motion, sliding across the floor and now out of direct sunlight generates shadow and confusion. Yoon runs after it, the Cowfish and Petod pursuing. The Doctor hits a door, knocking it aside and, as she passes it, Yoon reads the polished metal plate there. They are entering the Krodor section of the Embassy. This makes sense because Ibruk is a Krodorman, but also confirms a connection to the arrival of the Krodor ambassador here.

'Yoon!' She glances round. Two guards have brought down Petod and pinned him to the floor. She can hear the despair in his voice – the separation anguish – but best to get this done before the reaction becomes more organized. The remaining guard – the woman – raises her weapon, but the Cowfish barrels into her knocking her sprawling and comes on. The official just stands with his mouth open.

She follows the Doctor into the corridor beyond, seeing it take a turn at the end. Rounding that, she sees the Doctor sliding into a reception area almost as large as the foyer behind. Lights strobe and the sound of weapons fire reaches her a moment later. Shrugging under the impacts and expanding, the Doctor surges forward, but then a beam sears across, hot and high energy and the doctor retreats, expanding the reach of its shadow, to confuse what lies beyond. Without instruction from her it emits chemical terror and, as she comes up behind it she sees it should not have.

Guards in the blue uniform of the Krodor military, and wielding energy weapons, have spilled out into this area. Now they are terrified and it will not be possible to reason with them. She mentally berates the Doctor but it is rebellious – the free will she gave it yet to dissipate. It desperately wants to get to a double door over behind these soldiers.

Yoon realizes she is now in the midst of a 'diplomatic incident'. It is not of great concern to her, but it will be to others and to the balance here between her people and the off-worlders. It occurs to her that perhaps this was Ibruk's aim? She cannot yet parse the reasoning but, nevertheless, the man lies beyond that door and she will have her accounting. With a gesture she brings up the Cowfish and with a thought propels it forward. It hurtles across the polished floor, expanding to spread its substance over a greater volume, and the soldiers open fire with guns that can harm it.

The Cowfish takes many severe hits before it reaches the soldiers. Yoon's Bosch are rugged, tough and dangerous and can survive injuries that would kill most humans, but they are not immortal. Flesh peels and breaks over the Fish's body, bones show through like the frame in an old sofa, and it leaks a trail of yellow fluids across the floor. Thrashing its wings, it sends soldiers tumbling. The attack, the shadows and the terror permeating the air are enough to test their discipline and resolve, and the Plague Doctor's subsequent attack is enough to break it. Most run, though one or two go through that door. Some drop to the floor curled up foetal, overloaded. A man and woman, weapons abandoned, hurtle screaming past Yoon. She tracks their course to other soldiers behind, being urged forwards by the official, but not yet able to overcome their fear, and walks to the door as the Plague Doctor tears it off its hinges. Glancing over at the Cowfish, she sees it down and unable to pull itself back together, smoke and steam boiling from its flesh. It looks appeal at her and she pauses to lay a hand on pallid skin. Assimilating the correct toxins, she stabs in her claws and injects. Completion is not possible but she can at least give it peace. The toxins spread quickly and it slumps and, even as she steps towards the doorway, begins to come apart.

Within, a large stone slab table sits near the far wall, covered in soft screens Luxurious furnishings strew the area. A Krodor fig tree has grown around the walls. By the table stands a bulky Krodorman with soldiers either side of him. The Plague Doctor is on Yoon's side of the room, separated from the three now by monomesh screen that must have dropped from the ceiling moment's ago. The Doctor readies itself. The mesh will cause it damage but will not stop it from reaching its prey. She sends her thought, but the Doctor rebels because completion is so near. She pauses, strengthens that thought into command, stilling the Doctor, freezing it to the spot, then walks over to stand next to the screen, peering in at the Krodorman. He is clad in a suit resembling that of the ancient samurai of Earth, but completely grey and its sections of a softer material. He does not look as heavy as the Ibruk she last saw, perhaps because of the armour he wore then. His face looks thinner too, and there is not so much arrogance in his stance which, in the circumstances, is perhaps understandable. He wipes a hand over his polished opal skull and paces forwards to stand on the other side of the screen from her.

'Why do you do this?' he asks, concern and bafflement writ across his whorled features. In memory she sees him looming over her unclipping an armoured codpiece. She feels his weight crushing her and the pain, the fear and humiliation. But the weight of her mind entire pushes these aside.

'Why are you here?' she asks.

He grimaces. 'Politics. The old grew weak and ineffectual. We have fought a war and now the new replaces the old. Here where it has given too much ground to others I am properly establishing a Krodor presence.'

Yoon reaches out and touches one of the mesh filaments. It cuts into her fingertip. But for this everything would have been as intended. The Doctor would have reached this 'Ibruk' and he would have died.

'Your name?' she asks.

'Ibruk,' he replies.

'So it will be this "old" that wanted you dead?' she enquires. 'One with your appearance attacked me and left your seed.'

He is appalled, but rallies. 'A golem, a mechanism – they were used on Krodor during the war. Very dangerous. It will have a handler somewhere.'

'I apologise for my action here. My world will make restitution,' she says.

It is good that the last Batian did what he did and so alerted her to the possibility of this subterfuge. She looks round at those now gathered behind – Krodor soldiers, Embassy security, that official and others, Petod too – and nods. She heads away from the screen and takes a firm grip on the Plague Doctor's rebellious mind. As she walks towards the new arrivals it drags itself after her.

'We are going?' Petod asks, as a guard releases his arm.

Others mill about, but she can sense the orders being given and now they part ahead of her.

'We are going,' she affirms.

City police and Krodor soldiers. . . Petod watches the police move out across the churned terrain to head for the elevators and stairways leading up onto the spaceport platform. The cargo and passenger ramp leading into the city, forty feet up to his left, has been blocked by the soldiers. They even brought an armoured vehicle from somewhere in the city – a thing with twinned Gatling cannons apparently purchased from an alien race humans once fought.

'I thank you for your assistance,' says Yoon.

The police sergeant, recently departed from an armoured gravcar now resting on the ground behind her, is a big gruff woman. She rests a shock stick across her shoulder and tries to show confidence, but Petod sees she is in awe. It is notable too, he feels, that she is in command here, while the mayor and police commissioner are back in the city. Yoon's arrival here, the mayoral reaction and subsequent events at the Embassy have stirred up some big interests. The mayor, he understands, is now fighting for his political life, while all his hangers on are distancing themselves. Yoon's reminder has wrought change, which will, he thinks, be good, though he is in no way confident.

'Good to be doing something . . . positive,' says the woman.

'Catching criminals?' Yoon suggests.

The woman grunts an acknowledgement. As Petod reads it she was demoted because of her objections to the mayor's use of the police force as his personal army. Embassy interests put her in charge here, not least the Krodor ambassador now very definitely making his presence felt.

'So the subterfuge was to get you to attack and kill the ambassador,' she says. 'That does make sense because the security in the Embassy is strong and any other attack likely to fail. The Ibruk – the version of the ambassador that attacked you – is a golem?'

When they got back to the apartment – escorted by Embassy security and Krodor soldiers, shortly joined by city police – Petod viewed the file, dispatched by the Krodor ambassador, of one of these machines. The ancient design had once been the shell for an artificial intelligence. The Krodor used a control mechanism run by a handler. He, and Yoon, also looked at other files on albino ophidapts, all assassins.

'She could be any of them,' Yoon had said, on viewing the last. 'It does not matter for our purposes.'

'Where do we look now?' he had asked.

'There is one place left. I want you to check spaceship itineraries.'

And now they are here.

'All this is true,' Yoon replies to the sergeant.

'And our job is search and containment?'

'Yes.'

Yoon now points to the stair ahead and the platform undershadows. Out of that darkness the Plague Doctor looms, and then flows up the stairs. She begins walking.

'You know the ships to search and, when you find them, you leave the rest to me,' she says, and leaves the woman behind her.

'Are you sure we will find them here?' Petod asks, moving up beside Yoon.

'The assassin's expectation was that I would kill the ambassador,' she replies, 'whereupon my involvement would be at an end and she could leave in the resultant chaos. Now she cannot. And now she knows I am coming for her.'

As they reach the stair, Petod glances back. The sergeant's car is now in the air and heading to the platform to direct operations up there. They climb, finally stepping out onto metal gratings. Though he has spent many years in the city, Petod has never been here and only seen it this close in images. To his right he can see the mountains of the nearest Spineland, to his left run the lower slopes to one of the chains of lakes. The view is little different to that from the city wall, so he concentrates on his immediate surroundings.

Many ships rest here surrounded by refuelling and maintenance paraphernalia. He watches policemen entering via the cargo ramp of one vessel and others moving elsewhere to search the area. The Plague Doctor crouches in shadow at the base of a crane, having no scent trail to follow. Yoon moves on, inspecting each ship in turn and, intermittently, the Doctor catches up, sliding to the next patch of shadow. They come to a ship on the list – a thing like the block of some ancient piston engine – no police here yet. The Doctor moves in closer to a point between them and the vessel, looming by a stack of plasmel barrels.

He gestures towards the ship. 'Do we search or do we wait?'

'We wait,' Yoon replies, head moving like a searchlight as she checks around her, puzzlement writ on her face.

Police depart the ship they first entered and now head towards them. He looks around for the sergeant and, though he cannot see her, sees her car over by another ship.

'I don't suppose –' he begins, then sees a figure striding fast and confidently from the nearby ship towards them.

'Yoon,' says this man. 'So good to see you recovered!'

Yoon hisses, dropping into a crouch, while Petod gazes at the double of the Krodor Ambassador. This Ibruk raises his hand and the black object there cracks two times. He sees Yoon stagger, flesh and blood exploding from her back and feels something clip his trousers. She turns her face aside, coughs blood, then looks forward again as like some great black bat the Plague Doctor falls on the golem. The gun skitters away, claws rip in a morass of shadow. The fight is difficult to follow. He sees briefly a stone skull and shreds of unbleeding flesh and skin. Yoon stands and steps forward and he sees the wounds in her back easing closed. Something coughs like a giant clearing its throat. An acrid scent fills the air, and he realizes that the Doctor and Yoon, in this place, is the intent.

Then comes detonation.

Fire erupts from the throat of a steering thruster in the side of the ship, the blast wave hurling him to the ground in a shower of hot cinders. Burning barrels tumble past crumping heavily in their course and he sees one crash against Yoon to send her sprawling. The blast turns to a howl. He squints into the glare. Is it the engine flame howling or that staggering human figure – the last of its artificial skin burning and peeling, silver metal running as it collapses to scrap? Or is it the Plague

Doctor standing in the flame path, fighting what should have blown it from the platform, and then him and Yoon, for it blocks the blast? He sees the creature spreading – a sheeted mass folding out but failing, incandescent light glaring through its substance. It turns its weird birdlike head towards him and he knows what he must do. He rolls towards the sprawled form of Yoon, grabs her and hauls her up with a strength he never knew he possessed, throwing her more than human weight over his shoulder and staggers away. At last the Doctor fails, exploding away in burning tatters and the flame scores past them setting their clothing smoking. The ship moves as he drops with Yoon down by a stack of crates. It slides away from them, clips the edge of a crane and then shoots off over the edge of the platform, speeding away close to the surface of the world.

'Damn you,' whispers Yoon, abruptly sitting upright.

She straightens out a broken arm with a cracking sound, looks to Petod, exposing a face burned down to the bone on one side. She hauls herself to her feet slapping out smouldering fabric and peers up at the sky, contemplatively for a moment, and then nods her head.

Light spears down to hit the ship, and vomiting fire it drops. It hits the lower slopes, bounces up again shedding debris, and then skids out across the surface of one of the lakes. Its grav engine is still functional enough to give it negative buoyancy for a moment, but then something blows out of its side with a blue flash, and it begins to sink. Yoon grabs his shoulder and turns him, pointing him towards the sergeant's car.

'Come.'

Pain suffuses her body. The barrel broke her arm, crushed ribs already broken by the shots that also damaged organs, while the fire seared her to the bone. But the pain of the Plague Doctor's death also still cycles in her mind from a connection she could not close. She waves Petod to the driving seat and climbs into the other, ignoring the police and their sergeant running towards her. She feels a deep frustration with the messiness of her intervention here, at the incorrect deaths of two Bosch, at the chaos and lack of control. And at last her whole self is truly angry.

Petod lifts the car from the platform and sends it out towards the low slopes and lakes while she struggles to bring herself to order. Eventually, as they slide above the lake in which the ship sank, she restores a degree of equilibrium that manages to kill the pain.

'So what now?' he asks.

What now indeed. She studies him for a long moment, then makes the required changes inside herself – generates the required pheromones to her leaking skin. Next, she loads another complex organic chemical in the sac below the claw of her right forefinger.

'What now?' she asks. 'Now I release you.'

She reaches across and puts her hand around the back of his neck, pulls him in for a long slow kiss, gently pressing the tip of her claw into his neck and injecting his freedom. He responds eagerly to the kiss at the beginning, but then passion begins to wane as her chemical hold on him fades. He pulls back and looks in her eyes.

'It was strong,' he says.

'Yes, and I should not have done it. You are free now.'

'You've given me free will?'

'I have.'

'Okay then.' He leans forwards and kisses her aggressively.

Finally she breaks the embrace, surprised he has not as aggressively rejected her. Perhaps there will be something here, but later, for now she has a chore to complete. She checks herself again, sure the required chemicals emit from her skin, opens the car door, and steps out into the air.

She falls fast and hard, hitting the water feet first and losing herself in a cloud of bubbles. Her first breath of water is painful, like drowning because it has been so long, and her burns ache with the slight brine of it. But soon the familiarity of her favoured element embraces her. She swims down but not far, because the top of the ship is only ten feet below the surface. The shot she ordered from the station has torn a gaping hole in its side. Sculling in the water before this she peers inside, knowing that the chemical spilling from her burns are spreading in a fast sub-molecular process and already their reach is as much as a mile from her now.

The hole opens into a bridge and two seats are there – neither occupied. The equipment here is burned and blackened, its circuitry destroyed by the ion charge of the blast from above. She searches for human remains, but can find none. Perhaps the intensity of the burn here completely destroyed the albino ophidapt assassin.

No.

A door to the rear opens with an explosion of bubbles and a figure shoots out. The woman is clad in a skin-tight suit, gel over her eyes, and she has the adaptation to breath underwater. Shock lines cut through the water from a projectile weapon, one slamming into Yoon's belly then out her back through were her right kidney would have been, had she been human. She writhes away and shoots up, grabbing the hole's edge, and flipping over it as further shots crack by, rattling her ear drums. Tensing, she closes the wound – later body repairs needed. The ophidapt swims out, perhaps expecting to find her dying here. Yoon propels herself down hard, slamming into the woman at the waist, and they tumble away from the ship. The gun falls through the water, but a knife flashes out, cutting up towards her chest. Yoon could writhe away, but perhaps lose her grip. She allows the knife into her body under her breastbone, then stabs in her claws, injecting poison. The woman replies with a bite, sinking fangs into her neck.

Both of them now slow, fighting poisons as they float towards the surface. Yoon can see that what should have killed the woman instantly has not. Further extreme adaptations, but it is expected for a professional assassin to be difficult to kill. They reach the surface, floating just a few feet apart. The woman ejects water and gasps air.

'I should've . . . done the job . . . myself,' she says.

Yoon ejects the water from her lungs too, and replies, 'You would have failed.'

The woman contemplates this for a moment, then nods. She says, 'It's a mess, but I'll get clear of it.' She raises a hand out of the water holding another weapon.

'No,' says Yoon. 'You're just going to die.'

'Really?' says the woman, enjoying her power, enjoying the moment before the kill. 'How's that going to happen, then?'

Yoon sculls back from her, moving clear, and points past her. 'Like this.'

The woman turns, just in time to see the huge fin of the Progenitor cleaving towards her. The next moment she shrieks, travels twenty feet through the water sideways, a hot beam sawing away from her new weapon. Next, tugged from below, she disappears from sight. Yoon continues to scull, watching the spot as the red rises and spreads.

'Can I take you anywhere?' asks a voice above.

She looks up at the hovering gravcar, Petod leans out of the door and reaches down towards her. She stretches up and touches his hand for a moment. Smiles.

'Sometime soon,' she says, and dives down into healing waters.

ENDS

Printed in Great Britain
by Amazon